THE RETURN OF THE
KILLER CAT

By the same author

The Diary of a
Killer Cat

Notso
Hotso

Jennifer's
Diary

ANNE FINE

The Return of the Killer Cat

Pictures by Steve Cox

Farrar, Straus and Giroux
New York

Text copyright © 2003 by Anne Fine
Pictures copyright © 2003 by Steve Cox
Printed in the United States of America
First published in Great Britain by the Penguin Group, 2003
First American edition, 2007
1 3 5 7 9 10 8 6 4 2

www.fsgkidsbooks.com

Library of Congress Cataloging-in-Publication Data
Fine, Anne.
    The return of the killer cat / Anne Fine ; pictures by Steve Cox.
        p.   cm.
    Summary: Tuffy the pet cat narrates his escapades as he attempts
to escape his family's cat-sitter and suffers through a humiliating
episode of mistaken identity.
    ISBN-13: 978-0-374-36248-5
    ISBN-10: 0-374-36248-3
    1. Cats—Fiction.   2. Diaries—Fiction.   3. Humorous stories.
I. Cox, Steve, ill.   II. Title.

PZ7.F495673 Re 2007
[Fic]—dc22

2006041272

THE RETURN OF THE KILLER CAT

1: HOW IT BEGAN

Okay, okay! So slap my teensy little furry paws. I messed up. Big time!

And okay! Tug my tail! It all turned into a bit of a one-cat crime wave.

So what are you going to do? Confiscate my food bowl and tell me I'm a very bad pussy?

But we cats aren't *supposed* to hang about like dogs, doing exactly as we're told, and staring devotedly into your eyes while we wonder if there is some slipper we can fetch you.

We run our own lives, we cats do. I

like running mine. And if there's one
thing I can't stand, it's wasting the days
and nights when the family is on vaca-
tion.

"Oh, Tuffy!" fretted Ellie, giving me
the Big Farewell Squeeze. (I gave her the
cool blink, which means: "Careful, Ell!

Stay on the right side of cuddle here, or you'll get the Big Scratch in return.") "Oh, Tuffy! We'll be away for a whole week!"

A whole week? Magic words! A whole week of sunning myself in the flower beds without Ellie's mother shriek-

ing, "Tuffy! Get out of there! You're flattening whole patches!"

A whole week of lolling about on top of the TV without Ellie's father's endless nagging: "Tuffy! Move your tail! It's dangling over the picture!"

And, best of all, a whole week of not being scooped up and shoved in Next-door's old straw baby basket and stroked and petted by Ellie and her soppy friend Melanie.

"Ooh, you are lucky, Ellie! I wish *I* had a pet like Tuffy. He's so soft and furry."

Of course I'm soft and furry. I'm a *cat*.

And I am clever, too. Clever enough to realize it wasn't Mrs. Tanner coming to house-and-cat-sit as usual:

". . . no, she suddenly had to rush off
to her daughter's in Dorset . . . So if you
hear of anyone who could do it . . .
Only six days . . . Well, if you're *sure*,

Vicar. Yes, well. So long as you're comfortable with cats . . ."

Who cares if the vicar's comfortable? I'm the cat.

2: HOME NOT-SO-SWEET HOME

Uh-oh! Mr. Fussbudget!

"Off those cushions, Tuffy. I don't think you're supposed to be lolling about on the sofa."

Excuse me! Had the vicar not noticed it was me he was talking to? So what was I supposed to be doing? Mopping the floor? Tapping away on the computer? Digging the garden?

"Tuffy! Don't scratch the furniture."

Hel-LO? Whose house? His? Or mine? If I want to scratch furniture, I'll scratch it.

Worst of all: "No, Tuffy! I'm not open-

ing a fresh can until you've finished this."

I took a peek at "this." It was hard. It was lumpy. It was yesterday's grub.

And I wasn't eating it.

I walked away. The last thing I heard was Reverend Barnham calling after me: "Come back and finish your dinner."

In his dreams! I was off and out. I met up with the gang—Tiger and Bella and Pusskins—and told them I hadn't had dinner. They were hungry, too, so we sat on the wall and had a bit of a yowl about where to eat.

"Fancy peeling the pepperoni off a leftover pizza?"

"Fish without chips?"

"I could murder a nice bit of steak."

"Who's thinking stir-fried beef strips with scraped-off soy?"

In the end we went Chinese. (Love those ducks' feet!) Tiger strolled off on a smell tour down the alley to find the right place, and then we played Rip the Bags. (We all won that one.) Before you knew it, it was a pleasant dinner on the wall.

"Very tasty."

"Excellent."

"Nice choice. We must remember to eat here more often."

"And generous portions. Here is a family not afraid to waste food properly."

Unlike my friend, the vicar. Next morning, he was still shoving the dried-up grub in front of me. "Tuffy, I'm not

opening a fresh can. If you were truly hungry, you'd eat this."

Oh, would I? I didn't think so.

While he was waiting, the vicar stared out the window. "Look at that mess in the garden! Greasy paper wrappings! Ripped-up takeout food cartons! And that awful yowling kept me awake for hours. Don't think I'm letting you out again tonight."

I might be deaf to nagging, but I have ears. Thanks for the warning, Reverend! I crept upstairs and patted at the latch on the small bathroom window until it was the way I like it: far enough down to look as if it was still closed from yesterday; far enough up for one good paw push to open it.

As for that mess in the garden—don't knock it! It was breakfast.

3: MISTAKE!

Okay, okay! So it was a bit mean to hold that night's Talent Contest right under the vicar's bedroom window. Bella sang "Beoooo-ooooooooooooooootiful Dreeeeeamer." Tiger sang "Rolling Along to New Orleeeeeeeeeeeeans." Pusskins did his "Yodeling Song," and I did my brilliant imitation of Ellie when the car door slammed on her finger.

Still, no need for the vicar to get his knickers in such a twist. "If I catch a single one of you, I'll have your guts for garters!"

I didn't come home early. But everyone needs their sleep, so in the end the gang and I split up, and I strolled back. It was a beautiful morning. The only thing spoiling it was his voice. I could hear him three streets away.

"Tuff-eee! *Tuff*-eeee!"

I crept along in the shadow of Next-door's hedge. Melanie was leaning over it. "Please, Reverend Barnham," she interrupted him. "Does praying *work*?"

He stared at her as if she'd asked him something like, "Do trains eat custard?"

Melanie tried again. "You're always saying to people, 'Let us pray.' Well, does it work?"

"Work?"

"Yes. Do people get what they pray for? If I prayed really, really, really hard for something, would I get it?"

"What sort of thing?" Reverend Barnham asked her suspiciously.

Melanie clasped her hands together. "A pet all my own to cuddle. A pet who is soft and furry and warm, just like Tuffy behind the hedge here."

Well, thank you, Melanie! I took off, fast. And he was chasing me. That's why, instead of going up the apple tree as usual, I took that flying leap onto the handle of the lawn mower, and then up into the pear tree.

But when you get to the top of that, you find you have only two choices:

1. You can jump from the top branch

through a closed and locked bathroom window. (Uh-oh! My best escape route revealed!)

2. Or you can go back down, then jump from the lowest branch back onto the mower handle, and down onto the grass again.

Which—since my flying leap upward had flicked the power switch and started the mower spinning—turned out to be impossible as well.

4: STUCK UP THE TREE

Give him his due, he tried every-thing. He cooed. He cajoled. He wheedled. (There's not much difference between cajoling and wheedling, except wheedling's more whiny.)

Then he tried threatening. "You'll miss your dinner, Tuffy." (Scarcely a threat to make me tremble, given what was on offer.)

Then simple nastiness. "You can stay up that tree till you rot, Tuffy!" (Charming.)

The fact is, I wasn't faking it. I was dead stuck. Don't think I would have

chosen to spend half of my morning on one side of the tree, listening to him getting grumpier and grumpier . . .

"Come down at once, Tuffy! Get down here!"

. . . and the other half on the other side, listening to Melanie on her knees, with her hands together and eyes closed, praying and praying . . .

"Oh, please, please send me something soft and furry, just like Tuffy next door, to put in my straw basket and cuddle. I'll give it my comfiest pillow to sleep on, and feed it fresh tuna and cream."

Fresh tuna! Cream! Didn't the little lady know I had missed my breakfast?

Cat

bend under

ve given the

After a while, I couldn't stand listening any longer. I moved back to the other side of the tree. (Who could blame me?)

The vicar was clearly getting hungry, too. After a while, he stopped threatening me and went inside to make his breakfast. (No yesterday's grub for him, I noticed. Through the window came the sweet smell of sausages and bacon.)

They always say that breakfast is good for the brain. It certainly stoked up his little patch of gray matter, because a few minutes later he came down the garden carrying a stool.

And climbed on it.

And he still couldn't reach me.

I wasn't being difficult. I really wanted to come down. If he had managed to

But watching the branch
my weight did seem to ha
vicar an idea . . .

reach up even nearly hi
would have been prepared
his arms. (I might have so
little, but hey! Cats are fan
ungrateful, so why worry?

In fact, I actually tried
ing toward him along th

5: GENIUS!

He went inside the garage, fetched a length of tow rope, and came back under my tree. Climbing on the stool, he tossed one end of the rope over my branch.

"Right!" he said grimly. "Slipknot!"

I yowled. Was he planning to *hang* me? I don't often wish I could talk, but I admit that at that moment I wished I could rush back to the other side and drop a suggestion to Melanie: "Hey, sugar! Forget about praying for something soft and cuddly, and phone the cops. This vicar is trying to kill me."

He muttered his way through the slipknot. "Round and through, then round and through again."

(I kept up the yowling.)

He tugged the knot tight, then pulled on the rope. I dug in with my claws. The branch came down, but not quite far enough for him to reach me.

He tried again. This time, he managed to pull the branch a little farther down. (I nearly fell.) But it still wasn't quite far enough.

"Jump!" he said. "Jump the last bit, Tuffy!"

I gave him the blink.

"Jump, Tuffy!" he said again.

I glowered at him. (If you had taken a rolling pin to my eyes, and flattened them, they couldn't have gotten any

slittier. The look I gave him could have crawled through a closed venetian blind.)

"Chicken!" he said.

Okay, okay! So I spat at him. What are you going to do? Throw your woolly sweater at me? He called me a chicken!

He was practically begging for it. He as good as said, "Spit in my eye, Tuff!"

So I did.

He glowered back at me.

And then—oh, creepy, creepy! The glower turned into a little smile.

"A-ha!" he said.

I'll tell you something. People who don't really like you shouldn't say "A-ha!" It makes those who know they aren't liked very nervous.

Especially if they're stuck up trees.

"A-ha!" he said again, and hurried back to the garage.

The next thing I knew, he was backing the car out. For one horrid fur-shivering moment I thought he was planning on knocking my tree down. But then he stopped, put on the brake, and got out again.

He stood at the back end of the car and knotted the other end of the rope around the bumper.

"Right!" he said, admiring his handiwork. "I think that's so strong it'll pull the branch down low enough."

I stopped my pitiful yowling. I suddenly had hopes of getting down before I died of old age in that tree.

To be honest, I thought he'd hit upon a brilliant idea to rescue me.

I thought the man was a *genius*. I was *impressed*.

6: YIKES!

Well, I should have seen it coming. Don't get me wrong. The plan went well at first. Hunky-dory. He got back in the car, turned on the engine, and drove away from the tree at almost no miles an hour—

—carefully—

—carefully—

—until the rope went taut. The branch went down as planned—

—lower—

—lower—

—until my way back to the ground

was practically a gentle downward stroll.

"Brilliant!" I told myself. "I can manage that. Leftover sausage and bacon rinds, here I come!"

And I picked my way down the branch—

—tippety—

—tippety—

—and that's when his foot slipped on the pedal.

The car shot forward. The rope snapped under the strain. The forked tree branch became a giant leafy catapult—

—and I became a flying cat.

Wheeeeeeee! Watch me go! I flew in

one beautiful rainbow-shaped arc right over the treetop. (I tell you, I wouldn't want to do it again, but the view from up there was spectacular. Spectacular! You could see as far as the electric plant.)

But, after that, of course, the only way was

d

   o

      w

         n.

7: SPLAT!!!

Splat!!!

Straight into Melanie's little straw basket.

Okay, okay! No need to sob in your pillow! I may have splatted some of the not-so-cuddly little creepy-crawly things that were scurrying about on the cushion. I didn't actually end up picking any tiny crushed corpses out of my fur; but still, it would amaze me if all those ants who saw me coming got away in time.

Hearing the *thwack!* of my landing, Melanie broke off her prayer. She

opened her eyes and, seeing me in her straw basket, looked up to heaven.

"Oh, thank you! Thank you!" cried Little Miss Stupid and Soppy. "Thank you for sending me exactly what I asked for—something all soft and furry to cuddle, just like Tuffy."

Just *like* Tuffy?

Did she think I was sent from heaven? How soft *is* this girl?

But hey! Let's not be nasty about Melanie. I could have fetched up in a lot worse places than a cozy soft cushion in a little straw basket.

She carried me inside and kept her promise. Cream! Tuna! (Were you expecting me to slide off home to nose through some three-day-old pellets of cat food?)

Then she sat down and stroked my fur while she chose a name for me.

"Pussywussykins?"

Sure, Melanie. If you want me throwing up on your pillow each time you say it.

"Little Baby Munchywunchykins?"

Just try it, and I'll scratch you. Hard.

"I know. I'll call you Janet!"

Janet? What planet is she from? For one thing, I'm a boy. And for another, have I—have you—has anyone, anywhere—*ever* heard of a pet cat called Janet?

But the cream was fresh. The tuna was delicious.

So Janet was staying. Oh, yes. Janet was warm, well fed, and comfortable.

Janet was staying.

8: SWEET LITTLE PUSSY

Go on, then. Snigger. So I looked a bit of a pussycat, wearing that lacy bonnet. And the doll's frilly nightie was too big for me. What are you going to do? Ban me from Fashion Week?

I had a good time being Janet. The meals came three times a day. (Three times a day! That nightie was headed for being a perfect fit anytime next week.) I had steak bits, haddock, lean chicken, sausage ends. You think of what you really love to eat most, and then imagine

soppy little fingers feeding you, mouthful by mouthful, and you'll see why I stayed.

The only problem was the endless yelling from next door.

"Tuffee! Tuff-*eeeeeeee*! Where ARE you?"

Melanie settled me back down comfortably in the straw basket, and stood on tiptoe to peep over the hedge.

"The vicar's still looking," she told me sadly. "Poor Tuffy! He's still missing. I hope, wherever he is, he's warm and dry and comfy and well fed."

I purred.

She turned back. "Oh, Janet! I'm so glad to have you."

She squeezed me so tight, I gave a little warning yowl. Not a smart noise to make, just over the hedge from someone looking for a cat.

His head appeared. "You've found him!"

I stayed well down in the basket. Melanie's kind, but she's not bright.

"Who?"

"Tuffy!"

"No. That was my own cat yowling. That was Janet."

"*Janet?*"

"She was a gift."

I'm glad that Melanie didn't say "a gift from heaven." That would have made

him even more suspicious. As it was, he narrowed his eyes at me.

Disguise! I thought, and simpered in my basket.

The bonnet and nightie obviously confused him a little, but he did have a go. "His face looks exactly like Tuffy's."

I purred in a friendly fashion.

"But Tuffy never made a noise like that."

(No. Not in *your* presence, Buster!)

The vicar's eyes gleamed. "Melanie," he said, "do you mind if I do one tiny little test to assure myself it's not Tuffy?"

He came through the gate and picked me up.

Talk about tests! Some have to walk through fire. Others are sent on seven-year-long voyages. Some have to go and

make fortunes. Others kill dragons, or
set off to find the Holy Grail.

Nobody's *ever* had a test like this.

He scooped me out of the basket.

He held me up.

He looked me in the eyes. (I didn't blink.)

He said, "Nice pussy! Pretty, pretty pussy!"

He said, "Sweet, sweet pussy!"

He said, "Who's a clever little girl pussy, then?"

And all I did was purr.

He put me back in the basket.

"You're right," he said to Melanie. "It isn't Tuffy. And I can't think why I ever thought it was in the first place."

Phew!

More cream. More tuna. Here we come!

9: SHOWDOWN!

Go on. Admit it. You wouldn't have gone home either. You would have stayed the whole week, just like I did, stuffing your face and getting fatter and fatter.

By Saturday night, I was as big as a barrel. There were splits down my seams. I was bulging out of the nightie.

And that's when the gang came looking for me.

They peeped in the basket.

"Tuffy? Tuffy, is that you?"

I was a bit embarrassed. I disguised my voice.

"No," I explained. "I'm Janet. Tuffy's cousin."

Bella stared at the fur bulges bursting through the nightie.

"So what happened to Tuff? Did you *eat* him?"

I gave her the blink. "No."

"So where is he?"

I shrugged. Maybe it was the most

energetic thing I'd done in nearly a
week. Anyhow, the seams of the nightie
split, and a whole lot more of my bulges
fell out at the sides.

"Doing a striptease, are you?" Pusskins said, then added rudely, "Fatso!"

That set them all off.

"Fur Ball!"

"Tub o' Lard!"

I narrowed my eyes. I made the tiniest little noise. The *tiniest*. Everyone said afterward that I was the one who started it. But I wasn't. It was hardly a hiss at all. It was more like a *purr* really.

I blame Bella. She should never have put out her paw and patted me. "Come on, guys! Until Tuffy turns up, let's have fun with this great furry beach ball!"

So I thwacked her.

So she thwacked me back.

And that's how the fight started. It was quite a big flurry, with flying fur and shreds of nightie floating all over. At one point, the bonnet ribbons nearly strangled me, but I wriggled free, and took all three of them on again.

But suddenly, with my disguise in tatters around the lawn, the jig was up.

"Hey, guys! It *is* Tuffy after all! It's Tuffy!"

"Yo, Tuff! At last!"

"Found you!"

And that's the moment Melanie came out to the garden, carrying my third meal of the day.

The others stepped back respect-fully.

"Fresh cream!" sighed Bella.

"Real tuna!" Tiger whispered.

"Lots!" said Pusskins.

But Melanie didn't put it down as usual.

"Tuffy," she said to me sternly, "what have you done with Janet?"

I tried to look all Janety. But without

the lace bonnet and nightic, it didn't work.

Melanie looked around. And, I admit, if you were expecting to find your precious new pet, it did look a bit bad.

Shreds of fur and nightie and bonnet all over.

"Oh, Tuffy! Tuffy!" she wailed. "You bad, bad cat! You've torn Janet to pieces and eaten her! You *monster*!"

The others turned and fled and left me to it.

"You monster, Tuffy! Monster! *Monster!*"

10: HOW IT ENDED

So that sort of explains what all the fuss was about when the car pulled up to the curb, and out spilled the family.

"Tuff-eee!" yelled Ellie, catching sight of me through Melanie's open garden gate. She rushed in to greet me. "Tuff-eee!"

Then she spotted Melanie, sobbing her eyes out.

"What's the matter?"

"Your cat ought to go to prison!" Melanie shrieked at her. "Your cat's not a cat. Your cat's a *pig*. And a *beast*. And a *murderer*!"

I went back to trying to look all sweet and Janety.

Ellie's eyes had gone huge. She looked at me sternly and her eyes filled with tears. "Oh, Tuffy!" she whispered, horrified. "What have you *done*?"

Oh, very nice! Aren't people in families supposed to stick up for one another? Charming of Ellie to believe the worst, just because her best friend was watering the lawn with her tears and there were bits of shredded nightie all over.

I was pretty put out, I can tell you. I stuck my tail up in the air and started the huffy strut out of there.

Wrong way! Straight into the vicar's arms.

"Gotcha!" he said, scooping me up before I'd even spotted him lurking behind the pear tree. "Gotcha!"

And that's how, when Ellie's mother finally strolled through the gate, she found the vicar holding me the

way that a cat lover doesn't hold a cat.

And staring at me the way a cat lover doesn't stare.

And saying things I don't believe a vicar ought to say.

Ever.

He won't be asked to cat-sit in our house again.

Anyone sorry?

No. I didn't think so.

Byeeee!